A gift given with

....

....

....

From:

....

....

....

HOW GOD CHANGES PEOPLE

Conversion stories from the Bible

Carine Mackenzie

Illustrated by Natascia Ugliano

CF4•K

Contents

Turn to God

When Jesus started his preaching ministry he told people to 'Repent'. This means to turn from sin and turn to God. Jesus' message to us today is the same. He is telling us to turn away from a life of disobedience to God and instead to give our lives to him. We are to trust in Jesus. Only by God's grace can a person's life be turned around. It is his love, power and mercy that make this possible. This turnaround, or conversion, is marked by sorrow for our sin and faith in the Lord Jesus Christ who died for sinners on the cross.

To be converted and to enter God's Kingdom, we need God's Spirit to work in our heart. He deals with each one differently. We read in the Bible of many people who were converted – some dramatically, some gently, some early in life, one man just before he died. We read of one man who turned back to sin, but was later wonderfully restored.

God wants all people to turn to him and to trust the Saviour Jesus Christ.

Faith at the Fig Tree
Nathanael: John 1

Nathanael heard about Jesus from his friend Philip. 'We have found the Messiah,' he told him. 'The person spoken of in the Old Testament is actually here – his name is Jesus of Nazareth.'

'Nazareth! Can anything good come from that wicked place?' Nathanael exclaimed in amazement.

'Come and see for yourself,' replied Philip. When Jesus saw Nathanael coming towards him, he announced, 'Here is an honest man. There is nothing false in him.' Nathanael was judged to be pure not because he was good on his own account, but because he had faith in the promised Messiah, the Lord Jesus Christ.

'How do you know me?' Nathanael asked.

'I saw you when you were under the fig tree,' Jesus replied. A fig tree was often a place where devout Jews went to pray.

Nathanael was impressed by Jesus' knowledge of him. 'You are the Son of God,' he confessed.

'You believe because I told you that I saw you under the fig tree,' Jesus said. 'But you will see even greater things.'

Sharing the Good News

Andrew: John 1

ndrew was a fisherman on the sea of Galilee. When John the Baptist started preaching, Andrew heard him with interest and became one of his followers.

One day John pointed out Jesus to Andrew and a friend, 'Behold, the Lamb of God.'

Andrew and his friend spent the rest of the day with Jesus. They realised that he was the Christ, the Saviour of sinners.

Andrew wanted to share the good news about Jesus and he immediately went to find his brother, Simon. 'We have found the Christ, God's chosen one,' he told him. He brought Simon to meet Jesus too. Jesus gave him a new name – Peter, which means a stone.

When a person comes to know Jesus for himself or herself, it is good to share the good news with others and tell them about Jesus.

Two Men Who Saw

James and John: Luke 5, Mark 1

James and John were brothers, both working as fishermen on the Sea of Galilee. They were in partnership with Andrew and Peter. All of them saw Jesus' great power over the fish of the sea, when Jesus caused Peter's net to fill with fish. James and John had to hurry to help him pull the catch to the shore.

Jesus saw them mending their fishing nets on the shore with their father, Zebedee. Jesus asked them to follow him and they immediately left their nets and their fishing business to become followers of the Lord Jesus.

From that day their lives changed. They became disciples of Jesus, accompanying him around the country, listening to his teaching and seeing his love and care for needy people. They had the privilege of being eye witnesses of many miracles performed by Jesus and even the transfiguration on the high mountain, when Jesus' appearance changed. His face shone like the sun and his clothes became shining white.

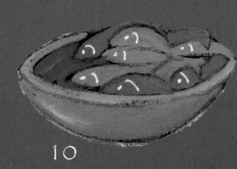

James and John faced difficulties too in their Christian life, but they persevered in the faith until the end.

A Fantastic Feast

Matthew: Mark 2: 13 – 17, Luke 5: 27 – 32

Matthew's life changed when he met Jesus. He was sitting doing business, collecting tax money for the government. As Jesus walked past his workplace, he called to him, 'Follow me.'

Matthew immediately left his work and followed Jesus. He became one of his disciples.

Matthew made a great feast for Jesus in his home, and invited many of his friends. Many other tax collectors and sinners met Jesus that day in Matthew's house. The Jewish leaders, called Pharisees, were annoyed to see Jesus mixing with these people.

'Healthy people do not need a doctor,' Jesus told them. 'Sick people do. I came to call sinners to repentance.'

When Matthew was converted, he wanted others to meet Jesus. When we come to trust in the Lord Jesus, it is good to tell others about him.

A Teacher is Taught
Nicodemus: John 3

Nicodemus was a religious leader in Jerusalem. He had heard of Jesus' miracles and one night, he came secretly to see him. He addressed him with great respect, 'Rabbi,' he said, 'you are a teacher come from God. No one could do these miracles unless God was with him.'

Jesus replied to Nicodemus in a startling way. 'No one can see the kingdom of God unless he is born again.'

'How can a grown man go into his mother's womb and be born again?' Nicodemus asked. But, Jesus was speaking about a different birth – a spiritual one.

Nicodemus was still puzzled. 'You are a great teacher,' said Jesus, 'and yet you do not understand these things.'

Jesus went on to explain how a man received this spiritual, eternal life. '*God loved the world so much that he sent his only Son into the world, so that whoever believes in him would not perish but have eternal life.*' Jesus Christ is the Son of God.

After that Nicodemus followed Jesus openly. At a council meeting some wanted to arrest Jesus. Nicodemus spoke up courageously, 'Does our law condemn a man before we hear from him? Surely not!'

After Jesus died on the cross, Nicodemus helped Joseph of Arimathea to bury Jesus' body. They took him from the cross and carried him to the tomb. They anointed the body with myrrh and aloes and wrapped it in linen. These loving actions by Nicodemus were evidence of the work of the Spirit of God in his life – he had been spiritually reborn.

Water for the Heart
The Samaritan Woman: John 4

One day Jesus was travelling on foot from Galilee to Judea. He went through the region called Samaria and because he was tired and thirsty he sat down at a well to rest. It was midday and they were near the town of Sychar, so his disciples went there to buy food. Jesus stayed behind.

An immoral woman came to the well for water. 'Will you give me a drink?' Jesus asked. The woman replied rather rudely. The Samaritans had a quarrel with the Jews and Jesus was a Jew.

However, Jesus spoke to her patiently and kindly. He explained that if she followed him, he would satisfy her longing heart even more than water satisfied her thirst.

Jesus knew all about her sinful life. He told her plainly that he was the Son of God. The woman believed him and her life was changed. She left her water pot at the well and went to tell other people about Jesus. 'Come, see a man who told me all I ever did. Is not this the Christ?'

Many believed on the Lord Jesus because of the woman's report about him and then because they heard Jesus for themselves.

16

They Fished All Night!

Peter: John 21, Luke 5

Peter and Andrew had fished all night and caught nothing. Then they saw Jesus on the shore. Lots of people were listening to him preach about God. Jesus stepped into Peter's boat and asked him to push out from the shore. He then preached from the boat.

Afterwards Jesus told Peter to let down his fishing net again. This time the net was so full of fish it almost broke.

When Peter saw Jesus' power he fell on his knees. 'Keep away from me, O Lord,' he said to Jesus, 'for I am a sinful man.'

Peter realised that he had a sinful heart and had done many wrong things. But Jesus did not turn away from him. 'Don't be afraid,' he said. 'From now on you will work for me.' Jesus chose Peter to be one of his special helpers, called disciples. 'Follow me,' he said to Peter and the others, 'I will make you fishers of men.'

Peter also realised that Jesus was the Saviour of sinners. When Jesus asked him, 'Who do you say I am?' Peter replied, 'You are the Christ, the Son of the living God.'

'My Father in heaven has taught you that,' said Jesus.

Just as God showed Peter he was a sinner and taught him who Jesus was, so he can teach us.

One Man Up a Tree
Zacchaeus: Luke 19

Zacchaeus was a tax collector – not at all popular with the people in Jericho because he was a cheat, taking more money than was due to the government and keeping it for himself.

One day Zacchaeus heard that Jesus was in town. Crowds of people lined the streets to see him. Zacchaeus wanted to see Jesus too, but he was not tall enough to see over the heads of the crowd. He was so keen that he ran along the road a bit and climbed up a sycamore tree to get a good view.

Jesus looked up at him, 'Hurry down, Zacchaeus,' he said, 'I want to come to your house today.'

Zacchaeus was delighted and came down at once. When the people saw what happened, they grumbled, 'Jesus has gone to be a guest of that sinner.'

Could Jesus change someone who was such a bad man? Of course.

'I will give half of my wealth to the poor,' Zacchaeus told Jesus. 'If I have cheated anyone, I will give back four times as much.'

Jesus said, 'Salvation has come to this house today. The Son of Man came to seek and to save the lost.'

The good news of the gospel is for sinners. Christ died for the ungodly.

I Don't Know the Man!

Peter: Matthew 26

Peter was often too sure of himself. 'I will never be ashamed of you,' he boldly told Jesus, 'even if everyone else is.'

But Jesus knew him better. 'Before the cock crows,' he said, 'you will deny three times that you know me.'

Later that night Jesus was arrested. Peter followed at a distance to the High Priest's palace. A girl spoke to him, 'Did you not go about with Jesus of Galilee?'

'I don't know what you are talking about,' he replied.

Another girl said, 'This fellow was with Jesus of Nazareth.'

'I don't know the man,' Peter declared. Then a man said to Peter, 'Surely you are one of Jesus' followers. You speak just like them.'

'I do not know the man,' said Peter roughly. Immediately the cock crew.

Peter remembered what Jesus had said. He had denied his Master.

He went outside and wept bitterly.

Peter had backslidden. He had been proud and self-assured and had fallen into sin. But Jesus does not reject those who love him and follow him even when they sin.

Remember Me!
The Thief on the Cross: Luke 23

It is best to trust and follow the Lord Jesus from an early age. But as long as a person is living, God's mercy is still offered. One man was converted and trusted in Jesus at the very last moment of his life.

When Jesus was nailed to the cross, two men who were thieves were also crucified, one on either side of Jesus.

One complained to Jesus. 'If you are really Christ, prove it by saving yourself and us too.'

The other thief was indignant. 'How can you speak like that? We deserve to die for our evil deeds, but this man has done nothing wrong at all.'

He turned to Jesus and said, 'Remember me when you come into your kingdom.' He realised who Jesus was – the mighty King.

Jesus gave him far more than he asked for.

'Today you shall be with me in heaven,' Jesus assured him.

This man was converted right at the end of his life and received God's salvation.

The other thief did not respond to Jesus. He died, as he had lived, an enemy of God.

Do You Love Me?

Peter: John 20 ~ 21

Jesus died on the cross, taking the punishment for the sins of his people. However, three days later he rose from the dead by the power of God.

After Jesus had died the disciples had been fishing all night, but had caught nothing. A man was on the shore watching them. 'Have you any fish?' he asked. 'No,'they replied. 'Put your net out on the right side of the boat,' he told them, 'and you will find fish.'

When they did this, the net became so full they could not pull it into the boat. 'It is the Lord,' John said to Peter. Peter jumped into the water, to get to the shore sooner.

Jesus had a meal of fish and bread ready for them. When they had finished eating, Jesus asked Peter, 'Do you love me?'

'Yes, Lord, you know that I love you,' Peter replied.

'Feed my lambs,' Jesus said to him.

Again Jesus said, 'Do you love me?'

'Yes, Lord, you know that I love you,' Peter answered again.

'Feed my sheep,' said Jesus.

Jesus asked the same question again, 'Simon, do you love me?'

Peter was upset at being asked a third time and said to Jesus, 'Lord, you know everything. You know that I love you.' 'Feed my sheep,' Jesus told him. Peter had now confessed three times that he loved Jesus. Perhaps he remembered with shame that he had denied Jesus three times in the past.

But Jesus had forgiven him and restored him and wanted to use him as a great preacher of the gospel.

Three Thousand Believe

Pentecost: Acts 2

Jesus had returned to heaven. The disciples were together at the Feast of Pentecost when suddenly they heard a strong wind. Tongues of fire rested on them and the Holy Spirit filled them with his power. The disciples spoke God's Word to the crowds in Jerusalem. There were many people there from other countries. Each man heard it in his own language. Some were amazed. But others made fun of them. 'They have had too much to drink,' they jeered.

Peter addressed the crowd. 'We have not drunk any wine,' he said. 'It is only nine o'clock in the morning.'

He continued preaching about Jesus, telling the people about his death and resurrection. He urged them to repent, to accept forgiveness of sin and to be baptised.

'What must we do?' they asked.

'Each one must turn from sin to God and be baptised in the name of Jesus Christ.'

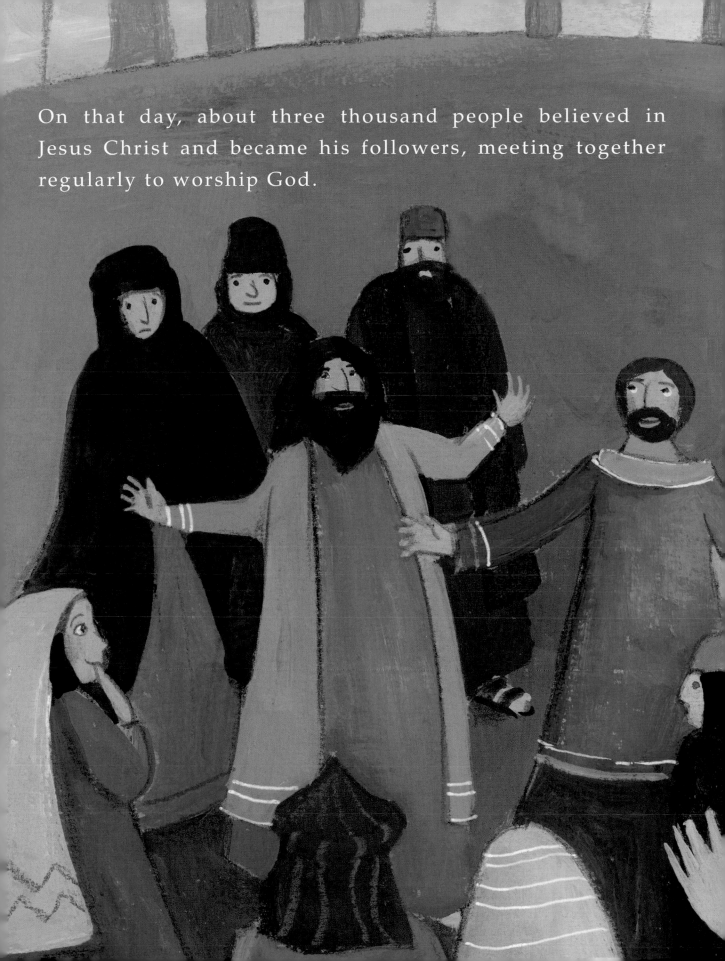

On that day, about three thousand people believed in Jesus Christ and became his followers, meeting together regularly to worship God.

Stop the Chariot!
The Ethiopian Official: Acts 8

Philip, a deacon from Jerusalem, preached about Jesus Christ to crowds of people in Samaria. One day an angel told Philip to leave Samaria and travel south to a lonely road in the middle of the desert.

On this road an Ethiopian official was driving in his chariot. He was returning home from Jerusalem where he had been worshipping in the temple. Philip was guided by God to approach the chariot. He heard the man reading aloud from a scroll of the book of Isaiah.

'Do you understand what you are reading?' asked Philip.

'How can I,' he replied, 'unless someone explains it?'

He was reading the part in Isaiah 53 that refers to a man who was led like a lamb to the slaughter.

'Who does Isaiah mean by that?' the Ethiopian asked. 'Is he speaking about himself or someone else?'

Philip explained that Isaiah was speaking about the Lord Jesus, the Lamb of God, who willingly died on the cross so that his people would be forgiven for their sins.

The Ethiopian then called out, 'Look, over there is some water. Why shouldn't I be baptised?'

'If you believe with all your heart, you may,' said Philip.

'I believe that Jesus Christ is the Son of God,' he declared. 'Stop the chariot.'

He was now trusting in Jesus Christ and what he had done on the cross. Both men went down to the water, and Philip baptised the Ethiopian. The Ethiopian went home full of joy.

Drama in Damascus
Saul: Acts 9

Saul hated Jesus and his followers. He dragged men and women from their homes and threw them into prison. He stood by and watched when Stephen was stoned to death for preaching about the Lord Jesus.

Saul, full of hatred to the disciples of the Lord, went to the high priest and asked permission to go to Damascus. His plan was to arrest the Christians who lived there and take them back to Jerusalem for punishment.

However, on the road to Damascus, Saul's life was dramatically changed. He was converted. A bright light shone from heaven with a blinding flash. He fell on the ground and heard a voice saying, 'Saul, Saul, why are you persecuting me?'

'Who are you, Lord?' Saul asked.

'I am Jesus, whom you are persecuting,' came the reply.

'What do you want me to do?' Saul responded trembling.

'Go to Damascus,' the Lord replied, 'and you will be told what to do.'

Saul got up and opened his eyes. He could see nothing. He had to be led by the hand into Damascus. For three days he was blind. He did not eat or drink anything.

Dreaming in Damascus
Saul: Acts 9

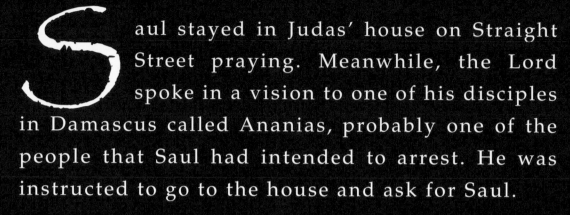

Saul stayed in Judas' house on Straight Street praying. Meanwhile, the Lord spoke in a vision to one of his disciples in Damascus called Ananias, probably one of the people that Saul had intended to arrest. He was instructed to go to the house and ask for Saul.

Ananias was reluctant. 'I have heard lots of bad reports about this man,' he objected. 'He has come here to arrest your people.'

'Go,' the Lord repeated. 'This man has been chosen by me to tell both the Gentiles and the Jews about me.'

Ananias went to the house. He placed his hands on Saul. 'Brother Saul,' he said, 'the Lord Jesus, who appeared to you on the road, has sent me to you so that you may see again and be filled with the Holy Spirit.'

Immediately Saul could see. He got up and was baptised. He then ate some food – the first for three days – and soon felt strong.

Preaching and Plots

Paul: Acts 9

The change in Saul's life was dramatic. No longer persecuting Christians – instead he had fellowship with them. He preached in the synagogue telling everyone the good news about Jesus, that he is indeed the Son of God. Paul's preaching about Jesus became so fervent that the Jewish people became really upset. They planned to kill Saul, but news of this plot reached Saul and his new Christian friends. One dark night they helped Saul escape by lowering him down in a basket over the city wall.

Saul's life was dedicated from then on to passing on the good news about Jesus and setting up churches in many places. He was a missionary; travelling round the countries bordering the Mediterranean as far as Athens and Rome – encouraging and teaching. When he could not visit, he sent letters to the churches, instructing them and correcting them.

At the start of this new life of service to God, his name was changed from Saul to Paul.

A Wide Awake Dream

Cornelius: Acts 10

Cornelius, a Roman army officer, lived in the town of Caesarea. He prayed to God and was kind to the poor. One afternoon while wide awake, he had a vision. He saw an angel who said, 'Send to Joppa for Peter to come to your house.'

Cornelius sent two servants and a soldier to find Peter. When they arrived, Peter was on the rooftop thinking about a vision he had received from the Lord. God, the Holy Spirit, instructed Peter to go with these men. Cornelius was waiting for them. A large group of his friends and family had gathered to meet Peter.

Peter explained that Jesus has followers from every nation. He told them about Jesus' miracles, his death and resurrection. 'Everyone who believes in him will have their sins forgiven through his name,' Peter declared.

God, the Holy Spirit, came with power and Cornelius and the others believed in Jesus Christ.

Jesus has followers all over the world. He has commanded all men everywhere to repent.

38

Her Heart is Opened

Lydia: Acts 16

Lydia was a wealthy woman who ran a business selling purple cloth in the city of Philippi in Greece. She was in the habit of going to the riverside just outside the city to pray on the Sabbath day with some friends.

Paul and his helpers came to Philippi and one Sabbath day made their way to the riverside where the women were praying. They spoke together and Paul preached, explaining the good news about the Lord Jesus Christ. Lydia responded to this gospel message. The Lord opened her heart and quietly she was converted and became a follower of Jesus.

She and her family were baptised. She persuaded Paul and his friends to come to stay at her house.

Conversion is a work of God's Spirit. God's Spirit worked quietly in Lydia's heart – enlightening her mind to know Christ Jesus and renewing her will to accept him, as she listened to the gospel being preached.

The fruit of the Spirit followed in her life – showing love to Paul and his friends, kindness, goodness, gentleness – in her hospitality.

A Quake and a Question

The Philippian Jailer: Acts 16

The jailer of Philippi had to make sure the prisoners in his care did not escape. His life depended on it. When Paul and Silas were thrown in jail because of their preaching, the jailer put them in a secure cell and fastened their feet in the stocks.

But Paul and Silas were very unusual. In the prison they praised God. All the other prisoners could hear them. Then at midnight there was a violent earthquake. The prison shook; the doors burst open, the chains broke loose. The jailer, in a panic, grabbed his sword and was about to kill himself.

Paul shouted out, 'Don't do it! We are all here.'

The jailer called for lights and trembling with fear, fell down before Paul and Silas in the dungeon. He took them out and pleaded, 'Sirs, what must I do to be saved?'

'Believe on the Lord Jesus Christ,' they replied, 'and you will be saved, and your family.'

Paul and Silas explained to the jailer and his family the good news of the gospel. They believed in the Lord Jesus and were saved. They were then baptised.

Timid and Trusting

Timothy: 1 and 2 Timothy

Not every conversion story is dramatic. When Timothy was a very small child, his mother Eunice and grandmother Lois started telling him stories and teaching from the Bible.

He learned the Scriptures from his earliest years and that made him wise to accept God's salvation by trusting in Jesus Christ.

Timothy grew up to be a missionary, travelling with Paul. He made special trips to Corinth and Thessalonica to help and encourage the Christian church there.

Timothy was naturally timid, but Paul encouraged him in the work of spreading the gospel. He was not a strong person, but Paul told him that training to be godly was more important than physical training.

Conversion is the start of the Christian life. We need God's grace every day to help us to cling to Christ Jesus and do what is right.

It's God's Work

You : Ephesians 2:8, 2 Corinthians 6:2, John 6:37

The conversion of a sinner is God's work. He deals with each person individually. Each Christian is given the gift of repentance from God, enabling him or her to turn from sin to God. They are also given the gift of faith. This enables them to trust in Jesus Christ for salvation.

It is important to realise that we are sinners and that Jesus Christ died to save sinners. Believing that, is the turning point in a person's life. This is conversion.

'For by grace you have been saved
through faith,
and that not of yourselves,
it is the gift of God.'
Ephesians 2:8

Love! Love! Love this book! Carine helps children see how God works salvation in many different kinds of people and that he can work salvation in them, too!

Connie Dever Wife of Mark Dever, Senior Pastor,
Capitol Hill Baptist Church, Washington D.C.

None of us are born Christians – we must be born again. Carine shows the need for repentance and faith in Jesus in each biblical story she recounts. How God Changes People will most certainly encourage children to think about what it means to be saved. The illustrations will delight their eyes, and the stories will delight their souls.

Keri Folmar Wife of John Folmar,
Pastor of the United Christian Church of Dubai

Carine retells what happened and happens when people meet the Lord. Engagingly written, and beautifully illustrated, How God Changes People is a book every family will enjoy.

Sinclair B. Ferguson, Senior Minister
First Presbyterian Church of Columbia

From the first picture, where even the robin looks startled at the sound of breaking glass, this is a lovely book for all ages. It cleverly brings together New Testament people who were changed by meeting Jesus. It quietly challenges the reader: 'Has He changed me yet?' It puts a hunger in their hearts to become part of Jesus' family.

Helen Roseveare, Author and Speaker

This book is a great reminder of people in the Bible who were completely changed by an encounter with Jesus. Beautifully illustrated, faithful to the Bible, and (refreshingly for a children's book) the stories are well applied.

Stuart Chaplin, Keswick 4 Kids Team Leader

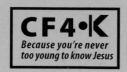

Christian Focus Publications publishes books for adults and children under its four main imprints: Christian Focus, Christian Heritage, CF4K and Mentor. Our books reflect that God's Word is reliable and Jesus is the way to know him, and live for ever with him.

Our children's publication list includes a Sunday school curriculum that covers pre-school to early teens; puzzle and activity books. We also publish personal and family devotional titles, biographies and inspirational stories that children will love.

If you are looking for quality Bible teaching for children then we have an excellent range of Bible story and age specific theological books. From pre-school to teenage fiction, we have it covered!

Find us at our web page: www.christianfocus.com

10 9 8 7 6 5 4 3 2 1

© Copyright 2012 Carine Mackenzie

ISBN: 978-1-84550-822-7

Published by Christian Focus Publications,

Geanies House, Fearn, Tain, Ross-shire,

IV20 1TW, Scotland, U.K.

Cover design: Daniel van Straaten

Illustrations by Natascia Ugliano

Printed in China

Scripture quotations are the author's own paraphrase.